Hanna-Barbera Authorised Edition

Yogi Bear & Giant Story Book

Written and Edited by Horace J. Elias

PURNELL

SBN 361 03165 3

Copyright© 1974 Hanna-Barbera Productions, Inc.

Yogi Bear: Oil Prospector copyright© 1974, 1969 Hanna-Barbera Productions, Inc. Yogi Bear and the Lost Raft copyright© 1974, 1969 Hanna-Barbera Productions, Inc. Yogi Bear and the Cranky Magician copyright© 1974, 1969, 1963 Hanna-Barbera Productions, Inc. Boo Boo and the Mysterious Guest copyright© 1974, 1969 Hanna-Barbera Productions, Inc. A Christmas Visit copyright© 1974, 1969, 1961, 1960, 1959 Hanna-Barbera Productions, Inc. Cindy Bear's Hero copyright© 1974, 1971, 1961, 1960, 1959 Hanna-Barbera Productions, Inc. The Jellystone Olympics copyright© 1974, 1971, 1961, 1960, 1959 Hanna-Barbera Productions, Inc. Show and Tell in Jellystone Park copyright© 1974, 1971 Hanna-Barbera Productions, Inc.

Published 1974 by Purnell Books, Berkshire House, Queen Street,
Maidenhead, Berkshire Under arrangement with Ottenheimer Publishers, Inc. Printed in the U.S.A.

Contents

Yogi Bear
Oil Prospector

Ranger Smith and Boo Boo, Yogi Bear's little chum, were sitting under a tree in Jellystone Park one day, playing 'Do you remember?'

The ranger had just remembered something funny that happened to him, when Boo Boo said, "Ranger, do you remember the time Yogi went prospecting for oil?" The Ranger laughed, but he hadn't laughed very hard when it happened . . .

What happened was this: Yogi and Boo Boo were out strolling in Jellystone Park one afternoon, when they came to a broad meadow. And standing in the middle of the meadow were two pieces of machinery.

"Gee whiz, Yogi!" exclaimed Boo Boo. "What's that funny-looking machinery doing here in Jellystone Park?"

Yogi said, "I heard Ranger Smith talking about it yesterday. I think they're going to open a new recreation area, and they're going to clear some ground and bring in a water supply. So they need the bulldozer — that's the yellow one with the sort of big shovel on the front — to clear the ground. The blue one digs a trench so they can lay some pipe under the ground to bring the water to where they want it!"

Boo Boo said, "Gosh, Yog — they're pretty big machines, all right! I bet they're hard to operate!"

"Naaahhh," said Yogi. "Nothing to it. All you do is climb aboard, turn the key to start it, pull the right levers, push the right buttons, and there you are! C'mon, I'll show you how!"

"Hey, no, Yog! I'm scared!" said Boo Boo.

"Scared of what?" said Yogi. "You just climb up on the bulldozer and I'll get on the trench digger. It's as simple as pie!"

Boo Boo didn't like it very much, but he slowly followed Yogi over to the two big machines.

"My goodness, Yogi," he said, "this thing's so doggone big I can't even climb up on it!"

"I'll give you a boost up," Yogi replied. And Yogi put his big paws together, Boo Boo stepped on them, Yogi heaved, and Boo Boo landed on the seat of the bulldozer!

"There you are!" cried Yogi. But Boo Boo still didn't like the whole idea.

"Yogi!" said Boo Boo in a very small, scared voice. "What do I do if this thing starts up?"

"Forget it!" said Yogi. "You can't start it — just keep your hands off the key, that's all!"

Then Yogi walked over to the other machine — the one which dug trenches. It had a big sort of wheel in front, with a lot of scoops attached to the wheel. When the wheel went around, the scoops dug into the ground and made a trench.

The big bear climbed into the driver's seat and looked around.

"How about this, Boo Boo!" called Yogi. "Some piece of machinery, huh?"

"Please, Yogi," begged Boo Boo. "Get me down from here! If the Ranger catches us fooling around with these big things, he'll run us so far it'll cost eleven dollars to send a postcard!"

"Just be patient a minute," called Yogi. "I want to try something!"

"Don't try ANYTHING!" yelled Boo Boo. "Let's just get off these things and away from here!"

"Be with you in a jiffy!" shouted Yogi — and turned the key! With a roar, the trench digger's engine started up. Yogi moved a lever — and then —

"Yippee!" yelled Yogi. "Here I go, Boo Boo!"

"Oh, no!" wailed Boo Boo, as Yogi started off in the trench digger. The big wheel was racing around, too — but Yogi hadn't moved the *other* lever — the one which lowered the wheel and started the scoops digging!

Yogi drove around in big circles in the meadow, yelling like a wild man. Everytime he passed Boo Boo, he gave an extra loud yell.

"Yogi! Be careful!" yelled Boo Boo. But with all the noise Yogi's big machine was making, there was no way Yogi could hear. Finally, however, Yogi decided it was about time to stop. He steered the trench digger in a few more loops, and finally pulled it to a stop. Then he turned off the key, and looked at Boo Boo.

"Hot dog!" said Yogi. "That's some machine! Boy, would I like to run that thing every day, and dig with it! You could dig up all kinds of stuff! Who knows? You might even strike —" Yogi stopped. Then he got a very strange look on his face.

"Yogi! Would you please help me down off this machine?" begged Boo Boo.

"Quiet! I'm thinking! Let's see now — do you suppose —?"

"YOGI!" shouted Boo Boo. "GET ME DOWN FROM THIS DOGGONE THING!"

Yogi looked around and said, "Huh?"

"Me, Yogi!" said Boo Boo. "Me, YOUR FRIEND, Boo Boo. Up here. GET ME DOWN!!"

"Oh, for gosh sakes, Boo Boo!" said Yogi. "What are you doing way up there?"

"You *put* me way up here!" screamed Boo Boo.

"Oh! So I did, didn't I?" said Yogi. "I guess I'll just have to get you down, then, won't I?"

16

And the big bear put his paws together, and Boo Boo climbed down. Then he just stood there and watched Yogi.

Yogi walked back and forth for a while with his paws behind his back. He was saying all sorts of things, but they didn't seem to make much sense. He said things like, "Suppose I — " and "How about if — " and "If the Ranger ever — " and "I think right here might be — ", and a lot more. Most of it he said to himself, so Boo Boo just heard a word every now and then. Finally Boo Boo ran out of patience and said, "Yogi, old buddy, will you please stop that walking up and down and talking to yourself? Have you got a stomach ache or something? Besides, it's getting dark. We've got a long way to go, and I'm getting hungry! Please, can we go back to the cave? Now?"

Yogi stopped walking up and down and looked at Boo Boo. Then he looked at the trench digger. Then he said, "Good!"

Boo Boo looked puzzled. "What does THAT mean, Yog? Do you mean, good, let's get back to the cave?"

Yogi said, "That means good! It's getting dark!"

Boo Boo said, "Sorry, buddy — you just lost me!"

"How would you like to be rich, Boo Boo," asked Yogi, "and help solve the energy crisis at the same time?"

Boo Boo said, "Huh?"

"Oil!" shouted Yogi. "We're gonna strike oil! Right here! Tonight!"

"You," said Boo Boo "are totally crazy! The Ranger will murdelize us!"

"If we strike oil?" said Yogi. "Oil? Right here in Jellystone? C'mon Boo Boo — it's dark enough now — let's get going!"

"Please, Yogi? Pretty please, with lots of sugar on it? Can't we go home? I'm tired and hungry and scared!" said the little bear.

"We'll eat later!" cried Yogi. "If you're tired, go under a tree and rest. And if you fall asleep, you won't be scared anymore!"

So that's what Boo Boo did. He walked to the nearest tree, sat down and went to sleep.

Yogi climbed on the digger, started it and moved the first lever. That started the big wheel racing round and round. When he pushed the second lever, the wheel lowered and began to dig, throwing dirt in the air as Yogi moved the big machine. Boo Boo was so tired even the noise didn't awaken him!

Yogi cruised the big digger back and forth over the meadow. He was absolutely convinced there was oil to be dug up — and he was going to find it! It got later and later, but Yogi didn't stop! He dug and drove back and forth, and to and fro, and Boo Boo slept on, sitting under the tree!

And then, just as the sun was coming up, something happened. Yogi was digging in the one place he hadn't dug before — in the very middle of the meadow.

Suddenly, there was what looked like a fountain in the meadow!

It gushed way up in the air, and Yogi promptly went wild with joy! He turned around and yelled at the top of his lungs, "Boo Boo! Wake up!"

He made so much noise that Boo Boo woke up at once. He yawned, stretched, then opened his eyes and looked! "Huh?" he said. "It must be a dream!" Then he ran as fast as he could to where Yogi was capering up and down, screaming, "OIL! OIL! I've struck OIL!"

Boo Boo stuck out a paw into what looked like a fountain. Then he licked his paw.

"Yogi," said Boo Boo. Yogi paid no attention to him. He kept right on jumping around, yelling "OIL! OIL! OIL!"

"Yogi," said Boo Boo again. "You haven't struck oil! You've struck WATER!"

"Water? WATER? You sure?" said Yogi.

"Taste it," said Boo Boo. Yogi did.

"OK," he said, "so it's water. But it's a geyser — it shoots up in the air! And they'll probably want to name it after me! You know — like that other one lower down in the park?"

"Hey!" said Boo Boo. "You mean Old Facefull? The one that shoots up every hour?"

"That's the one!" cried Yogi. "They have to call this one Old Yogi, won't they? I found it, didn't I? Maybe I was looking for oil — but a genuine, brand-new geyser's pretty good, too, isn't it?"

"I guess so," said Boo Boo, doubtfully.

"Look at that baby shoot up in the air!" said Yogi. "MY geyser! Old Yogi! Boo Boo, maybe I didn't strike oil, but I'm gonna be famous!" And Yogi danced around, splashing in and out of the geyser. After quite a little while, he looked around for Boo Boo, who came running out of the woods, calling to Yogi.

"Yogi!" called Boo Boo, when he was still a little distance away. "The ranger was here and — "

"The Ranger?" cried Yogi. "Gonna name it after me, huh? Couldn't wait, huh? What did he say, Boo Boo? I guess we showed him!"

"Well, not exactly," said Boo Boo. "He sent me back to tell you to get very busy with a shovel."

"I guess he's right," said Yogi. "I did make an awful dug-up mess around here. But what about the geyser — the new one I found? Wasn't he happy about that?"

"Not very," continued Boo Boo. "You see, the biggest tourist attraction in the park has stopped running!"

"Not Old Facefull?" gasped Yogi.

"Old Facefull," said Boo Boo. "When you opened up Old Yogi, that was the water that ran down to Old Facefull — and Old Facefull didn't get any more water — it's all shooting out up here!"

"So —," began Yogi.

"So —," said Boo Boo, "start shoveling, old buddy. You just had a bad night, I guess. No oil, no Old Yogi."

"Tough, huh?" said Yogi, as he started shoveling.

"Oh, well," said the young bear, "you've still got me — Old Boo Boo!"

Yogi Bear and the Lost Raft

The argument between Ranger Smith and Yogi was over a pair of galoshes. But it began the night before, when four campers found the Ranger and began to yell at him.

"Where's that miserable bear?" yelled one camper.

"He's run away!" hollered another camper.

"He stole our food!" bellowed a lady camper.

"And now we're lost!" wailed the other lady camper.

When Ranger Smith got them quieted down, he figured out what had happened. He had assigned Yogi to guide six people through the park, then take them down the river through the rapids on a raft. Yogi had started off with them. But then he disappeared with the raft — and their picnic hampers were missing, too! The next day, the Ranger found the other two people, who were just as lost, and even hungrier.

The Ranger sent out word all over the park: FIND YOGI AND SEND HIM TO ME! A little later that day, Yogi walked into the office.

"You want to see me, Ranger Smith?" asked Yogi.

"NO!" snapped the Ranger. "You're the *last* person I *want* to see — but I can't help it! I need you! Every guide in the park is either busy or sick. Now what did you do to those six people you were supposed to guide through the park?"

"I'll tell you what I did!" snapped Yogi, "I left 'em!"

"Why?" said the Ranger.

"Because they laughed at me!" said Yogi.

"I think I'm going crazy," said the Ranger. "Why did they laugh at you?"

"Because of those silly, stupid, gum-foozled galoshes!" yelled Yogi.

"Galoshes?" said the Ranger. "They laughed at you because of these GALOSHES?"

"That's right!" said Yogi. "Boo Boo said they'd laugh, and they *did*! I will NOT wear GALOSHES ANY MORE! EVER!"

"But Yogi!" said the Ranger. "They're only to wear to keep your feet from getting muddy! I can't have my guides running all over the park with muddy feet! That would look terrible!"

"They *laughed* at me," said Yogi. "Why can't I wear hip boots — the ones the fishermen call waders, like all the other guides? Why do I have to wear GALOSHES? Gosh, they make me feel like I was on the way to kindergarten with story books under my arm!"

"There's only one pair of waders left, and they're mine," answered the Ranger. "And I need 'em."

"That's all right with me," said Yogi. "You can have me *without* galoshes or *with* waders. I'm the only guide you have left. Take your choice!"

And Yogi threw up his hands and went out the door. Yogi didn't really care what the Ranger decided to do. He had other plans!

He hurried home and began packing. "How about you, Boo Boo? All packed?"

"Yep," said Boo Boo. "All ready to go."

"Good," said Yogi. "We wait a while, then we sneak off to where I hid the raft. Did you get the picnic hampers stowed away?"

"You bet!" said Boo Boo. "While you and the Ranger were arguing, I loaded them in the raft and covered 'em up!"

"OK!" said the big bear. "Let's go for a ride on the river, and have some good food for a change!"

"Say, Yog," said Boo Boo. "Why don't we leave the suitcases here, and check things out first? Let's make sure the raft is still there, and the hampers, too!"

"Good idea," said Yogi. "We'll wait until dark to leave. The Ranger might get suspicious if he heard we were sneaking around the park with suitcases!"

And that's exactly what they did. They went to the hiding place, located the raft and made sure of the hampers.

In the meantime, the Ranger had made up his mind. "I guess I'll have to lend him my waders," he said to himself. "It looks like the best way to keep everybody happy." And then he sent for Yogi, only to be told that Yogi had disappeared — and Boo Boo, too!

"Drat that bear!" said the Ranger. "Find him!"

At just about that same time, Boo Boo had an idea. "Yog," he said. "Have you ever ridden in one of these things?"

"Nope," answered Yogi. "Why?"

"Maybe we should sort of take a test ride to see how it goes," went on the little bear. "Golly, we don't even know whether it leaks!"

"Hmmm," said Yogi thoughtfully. "Maybe you're right." And he walked around the raft and kicked it a few times, like a grown-up testing automobile tires.

"Tell you what we'll do, Boo Boo," continued Yogi. "Let's push her out in the river, and ride a few hundred feet downstream. That way we can see how it handles, and whether there are any leaks!" And that's what they did — hauled it to the water, jumped in, and pushed off into the stream.

The little raft immediately started to spin!

"Hey, Yogi," cried Boo Boo. "Stop this thing from spinning! I'm getting dizzy and seasick!"

"I *can't* stop it!" yelled Yogi. "The doggone thing hasn't got any paddle!"

"Oh, no!" moaned Boo Boo. "You gotta get me out of here! I'm seasick!"

"That tree!" yelled Yogi. "I'll grab a branch, and you grab me!"

Yogi jumped and caught a branch. Boo Boo got himself together just enough to grab Yogi, and they both yelled as loud as they could for help.

Two campers and a fisherman heard them, and ran toward the noise.

While they were running to the noise, Boo Boo swung himself hard, let go and managed to drop to the ground. Then Yogi pulled himself up on the branch, walked to the trunk, and climbed down. Now that things had stopped going 'round and 'round, Boo Boo felt all right again.

"Boo Boo!" cried Yogi. "We've lost all that good food!"

"Can't be helped," said Boo Boo.

"Tell you what," said Yogi. "I'll wait for the Ranger. You hide, then start looking for that raft. I want those picnic hampers!"

"OK, Yog," said the little bear — and he did.

At this point, the campers and the Ranger came racing up to where Yogi and Boo Boo were sitting.

"OK, everybody, thanks for helping. You can go back now — I'll handle this!" said the Ranger. "All right, Mr. Smarty-pants bear — explain *this* one!"

"Well, it's really quite simple, Ranger Smith," explained Yogi with a very mischievous look in his eye. "We found the raft, and we were bringing it downstream to where we thought *you* were, and then it started to spin — By the way — how was I supposed to control it without even a paddle?"

"Never mind that!" snapped Ranger Smith. "Where is it now?"

"Where's what?" asked Yogi.

"The raft!" screamed the Ranger.

"Oh," answered Yogi. "The RAFT! Well, sir, last I saw of it, it was headed downstream. If we hurry, maybe we can catch up with it!"

"Let's go!" yelled the Ranger.

"Get a rope!" yelled Yogi. "If we find the raft, I'll swim out with the rope and you can haul it in!"

The Ranger quickly found a camper who lent him a long rope, and they raced down the river bank, looking for the raft.

On the way, Yogi passed Boo Boo, hiding in some bushes. "Pssstt!" hissed Boo Boo. "I managed to get one of the hampers out of the raft and hid it!"

"OK," whispered yogi. "Gotta go now!"

Finally, Yogi and the Ranger caught up with the raft, bobbing up and down out in the middle of the stream.

Yogi grabbed the rope and swam out to the raft. Just as he was ready to tie on, he thought, "Jeepers! There's a hamper missing — I can't let him pull the raft to shore!" So he just *laid* the end of the rope in the raft, hollered "Pull away!" swam to the opposite shore and tiptoed away.

Naturally, when the Ranger pulled on the rope, the rope just slipped into the water, and the raft kept right on going.

"Funny," said the Ranger. "That blasted bear's up to something again!" So he sent out orders to bring Yogi in once more. It didn't take very long to find him and bring him in.

"Yogi Bear," said the Ranger, "I don't know what you're up to, and I don't care. Get me that raft and those hampers!"

"I'll get my feet all muddy," said Yogi, in a nasty-nice sort of way.

The Ranger sighed, "Take my waders," he said, "but *bring 'em back*!" He stalked into his private office and slammed the door.

"Hot dog!" thought Yogi. "All that good food! I'll find that raft if I have to search all night!"

"Well, now!" he thought, as he left the Ranger's office, wearing the waders. "How can I work this out? If I find the raft and bring it back, there's a hamper missing — and the Ranger will be mad at me. If I *don't* find the raft and come back, he'll be even *madder*! So no matter what I do, I'm in the soup!" He thought some more, and then, "Suppose," he thought, "just suppose I find it — and *don't* come back! That way — I've got a raft, the food, the waders — by golly, that's it!"

It didn't work out quite that way, though. Yogi was up and down the river all day and half the night. He found an old rowboat with no bottom in it, but he never did find that raft.

He looked for Boo Boo, but he couldn't find him, either, because the little bear had hidden himself deep in the woods. After quite a while Boo Boo got very hungry, and decided he couldn't wait for Yogi any longer. And he ate all the food in the hamper.

Yogi finally gave up, went back, and told the Ranger all about what he'd tried to do. You can imagine how angry the Ranger was.

You can imagine, too, that it was a long, long time before Yogi tried anything like *that* again.

Yogi Bear and the Cranky Magician

At first Yogi Bear thought his eyes were deceiving him. Or perhaps hungry bears imagine they see food in front of them, like thirsty desert travellers see water where there is only sand. But when he looked again it was still there.

"Do you see what I see?" Yogi asked his friend Boo Boo. "Unless my eyes are playing tricks on me, there's a chock-full-of-goodies picnic basket just under that tree and it's sitting on thin air!"

"Let's run," said Boo Boo. "You know picnic baskets always get you into bad trouble. A picnic basket sitting on a table where there *is* no table surely means trouble!"

But Yogi felt brave as well as hungry, so he tiptoed into the clearing. But just as he was about to reach the basket he heard a sound. *Zop*! And the picnic basket suddenly disappeared.

"Look out!" Boo Boo cried.

Yogi spun around and saw a strange-looking man. He was dressed all in black and his white hair stood out angrily from under his top hat. His moustache was very black and it curled up in a very menacing way. He was carrying a cane that said on it: 'Magic — Handle with Care!'

"Pardon me," said Yogi, politely. "Have you seen a picnic basket? It was right here before my eyes just a second ago."

"It was up in the air, but it really was here! I saw it too," said Boo Boo.

"I made it vanish," said the man. "I am Abner K. Dabra, the Cranky Magician."

Yogi and Boo Boo looked at each other and grinned. A magician indeed! He couldn't fool them.

"I'm Yogi, the *Greedy* Magician," said Yogi. "I've made many a picnic basket disappear myself."

Boo Boo laughed.

But then, to show that he wasn't fooling, the magician did a cranky thing. He took off his high hat, gave it a nasty kick, and blamed his bad manners on the hat.

Yogi and Boo Boo watched him in amazement.

"That's pretty cranky, all right," said Yogi. "But are you a magician?"

For proof, Abner K. Dabra pointed his cane at a bird, a little brown bird who was merrily chirping. *Zop!* The song stopped abruptly as the bird disappeared. Then he pointed at a bee which had alighted on a flower. *Zop!* The bee disappeared too.

"Ho! Ho! But you're not the only magician in Jellystone Park," said Yogi. "Watch this disappearing act!" And he and Boo Boo ran like the wind before Abner could aim his cane at *them*!

After breakfast the next morning, Yogi went to his special resting tree for a nap. But what a surprise! When he leaned against the tree he fell flat on his back. It was gone!

Boo Boo came along to join Yogi, and they looked all over for the tree.

They looked under rocks . . . and behind trees . . . and even under Yogi's hat. But the tree was nowhere around.

"My detective-type brain tells me that this is the work of that cranky magician," said Yogi. "It has to stop."

Boo Boo agreed. If things kept disappearing like this, life could become very uncomfortable.

But what could they do? They couldn't work magic and they weren't fierce enough to frighten him, as some animals could have done.

"Let's go see the Ranger," said Boo Boo. "Maybe he can do something." So Yogi and Boo Boo started out for Ranger Smith's cabin.

But when they got to the place where the cabin had been, they found only a bathtub standing alone in an empty space with the faucet dripping.

Just then the Ranger came out of the woods, dressed in a bath-towel and looking very puzzled!

"I can't understand it," he said. "I was taking my morning shower when suddenly, *Zop*! my cabin vanished."

"It's Abner K. Dabra again!" said Boo Boo.

"He's a magician," explained Yogi. "He points his cane at birds and bees and cabins and trees and they just vanish into thin air. Do something, Ranger Smith, *please*! You're in charge here!"

Yogi and Boo Boo felt that everything would be alright now. The Ranger would see to it.

So the three of them went all around the park looking for the magician. When they found him, Yogi and Boo Boo hid in the bushes.

The Ranger went to tell Abner K. Dabra that it wasn't nice to point — especially with a magic cane.

But before he could say a word, *Zop!* he was gone. And Yogi and Boo Boo heard Abner K. Dabra say, "Now *I'm* in charge of Jellystone Park!"

And he looked crankier than ever!

Yogi and Boo Boo didn't wait to hear any more. They scampered away as fast as they could to hide in Yogi's cave.

"But we aren't safe from that magician, even in a cave," moaned Boo Boo.

"Now, stop worrying, Boo Boo," said Yogi. "We've got to think of a plan to outwit him."

"A plan," Boo Boo cried. "What good is a plan against his magic?"

"Don't despair," said Yogi. "There must be something we can do."

"It's up to us now," he added. "If we don't stop that magician, there won't be a thing of value left in Jellystone Park."

"Oh, woe is we," Boo Boo wailed. "No birds or bees or rocks or trees."

"And worse than that, no picnic baskets," said Yogi, pacing up and down as he became more and more worried.

"Think, Boo Boo, think!" said Yogi. "What can we do?"

Boo Boo stopped wailing. He had made up his mind. There was only one thing they could do.

"We can move," said Boo Boo, and he started to pack.

But Yogi stopped him. "No, we have to save Jellystone Park," he said. "And I know how to do it!"

So the two heroes set out to save Jellystone Park, Yogi marching bravely in front and Boo Boo following him fearfully.

They soon came within sight of Abner K. Dabra's camp and they crept quietly up to it. They saw the magician taking his afternoon nap. His coat was hanging on a tree limb and his magic cane stood nearby.

"Shh!" said Yogi. "This is our big chance, Boo Boo!"

Slowly and carefully, he tiptoed up to where the magician was sleeping. He picked up the magic cane, pointed it at him, and — *Zop*! Abner K. Dabra, the cranky magician, was gone!

Boo Boo rushed out of the bushes and danced with joy. "Hooray! You've done it, Yogi," he shouted. "You've saved Jellystone Park!"

Yogi felt like a hero.

They both felt very pleased and happy until, suddenly, Boo Boo thought of something that made him sad again.

"But what about the Ranger? I'll miss him."

Yes, Ranger Smith might be a nuisance sometimes — but they couldn't imagine Jellystone Park without him.

At that moment Yogi and Boo Boo heard a voice from the magician's coat. It was a cranky voice and it said, "It's crowded in here! Make room! Everybody make room!"

"I'd recognize that cranky voice anywhere," said Yogi.

Then he took the coat from the tree and began shaking it, and from the sleeves came everything that had disappeared.

Out came the picnic basket.

Then the bumblebee and the bird and the resting tree. And next came the Ranger's cabin.

And then — Ranger Smith himself.

"We should have guessed," said Yogi. "It's a well-known fact that magicians hide their loot up their sleeves."

He gave the coat another shake and — lo and behold! — out came Abner K. Dabra!

But he looked different somehow. He no longer looked angry or cranky; he looked frightened.

The cranky magician took a look at Yogi, who was still holding the cane, and began to run. He ran and he ran. The last Yogi and Boo Boo saw of him he was racing out of Jellystone Park.

And nobody was sorry to see *him* go.

"Thank goodness that's over," said the Ranger. "Now to put these things back in place!"

"Not so fast," said Yogi, eyeing the picnic basket. "I have one more trick of magic to do. Watch me, Boo Boo and Ranger Smith, *I'm* going to make that food disappear!"

Boo Boo and the Mysterious Guest

One morning in June, Boo Boo came out of the cave where he and Yogi Bear lived in Jellystone Park. He was just about to sit down and read the morning paper, when a car stopped and Ranger Smith jumped out. "Morning, Boo Boo!" he called.

"Morning, Ranger Smith!" answered the little bear. "What brings you out so bright and early?"

"Boo Boo, I've decided it's time you took some responsibility," said the Ranger. "I have a very important assignment for you."

"Gee whiz, Ranger," said Boo Boo. "What kind of assignment?"

"Tomorrow," went on the Ranger, "we are going to have a very, very important guest in the Park. And here is your assignment: I want the Park cleaned up; I want every bird and beast bright and shiny; and most important of all, tomorrow you will be the official host for our important guest!"

"I have to do all of *that*?" said Boo Boo. "Golly, Ranger there's not much time! And by the way — who's this important guest?"

"That," said the Ranger, "is something we won't know until tomorrow."

"If you don't know who the guest is, how do you know he's important?" asked Boo Boo.

The Ranger laughed. "We don't even know if it will *be* a 'he'," he said. "That's why we just have to wait until tomorrow!"

"Yessir!" said Boo Boo, and went to work!

He began by telling the birds to clean up their nests. But the birds nearly drove him crazy, demanding to know who the mysterious guest was. The bluejays and the purple grackles were the worst. The racket got so bad Boo Boo developed a headache!

"For goodness sakes!" he thought. "If I can't even get these goofy birds to go to work, how am I gonna get the whole Park straightened up?"

Then he thought of something. "When the Ranger wanted to get this job done," he said to himself, "he didn't go running around telling every animal and bird — he came to *me*! So why don't I do what the Ranger did?"

The next problem was who to give the job to. It didn't take long to figure *that* one out.

He walked over to a tall tree where one bird was sitting on a low branch. "Psssst!" he said.

"You talking to me?" asked the bird.

"Come on down," replied Boo Boo. "I need some help." The bird fluttered down and perched on Boo Boo's shoulder.

"What's your problem, Boo Boo?" asked the bird, whose name was Clyde Twitter.

"Clyde," began Boo Boo, "can you carry a message for me? It has to go to every bird and animal in the Park — and it has to get there FAST!"

"I guess so," replied Clyde. "I'm a pretty fast flyer, and I can holler pretty loud. Wanna hear me?"

"No!" cried Boo Boo. "I have a bad enough headache right now!"

"What's the message?" asked Clyde. And Boo Boo told him.

"How about those owls?" said Clyde.

"Hmmmm," said Boo Boo. "Yes. The owls. Tell you what — you get going. I'll handle the owls." And Clyde flew off.

This was the problem with the owls: they are *very* messy birds, they sleep all day, and they're hard to awaken. So Boo Boo decided to write a note and leave it at their home in a hollow tree. He got to the tree, climbed it and left a note. Then he slipped and fell out of the tree! He finally got up, dusted himself off and decided to walk around to see how things were going.

The first thing he saw was Clyde, up in a tree, bossing some woodpeckers, who were hard at work nailing down nests, burying trash and cleaning up piles of sawdust.

"Hey, Clyde!" hollered Boo Boo. "How's it coming? Did you deliver the message?"

"Everybody's working like a beaver!" shouted Clyde. "And the beavers are working twice as hard as anybody else!"

"Great!" called Boo Boo. "Keep up the good work!"

"Got one problem," called Clyde from his perch on the tree. "Everybody wants to know who the mystery guest is!"

"So do I!" replied Boo Boo. "We'll all just have to be patient until tomorrow! I'm going to check on the foxes and the field mice! See you later!"

Boo Boo continued his inspection. The beavers were cleaning up their dams, and washing themselves carefully. In a big meadow, the red foxes (who are very vain animals) were combing their long fur, and picking leaves and twigs and burrs from their big bushy tails. The field mice were where they belonged, (in a field, of course) and were doing something peculiar with spools of thread. Boo Boo saw that it looked pretty clean, so he didn't bother to ask them *what* they were doing.

Bees were everywhere, tidying up their hives and washing honey off themselves. Even the bears were working — grumbling about it, of course, because bears are very, very lazy and hate to work — but they *were* working.

"My goodness gracious sakes alive and then some!" exclaimed Boo Boo. "This Park is *jumping* today! Gosh, I sure hope this important, mysterious guest appreciates all the work going on around here! Golly Moses!"

Boo Boo continued to inspect the Park. Finally, when it was getting so dark that he couldn't see what was going on, he went back to the cave where he lived with Yogi. Yogi wasn't home at the time (he was off visiting some of his relatives in Canada) so Boo Boo slept alone.

The last thing he heard was an argument outside of his bedroom window. A red fox and a field mouse were making so much noise he couldn't sleep.

"Hey!" he called. "Go to bed, you guys! Big day tomorrow!"

"Who's the guest?" they said.

"GOOD NIGHT!" said Boo Boo, and went to sleep!

In the morning, Ranger Smith introduced everybody to Superintendent Simpson, who said, "Congratulations! I've never seen this park looking so beautiful and clean! Boo Boo, Ranger Smith tells me you're responsible for this! You've done a fine job, young man!"

Boo Boo was so proud he thought he'd bust wide open.
And then Yogi, who had returned from Canada during the
night, said, "I always told you he could do *anything,* if you
gave him a chance to do it!"

And then Ranger Smith said, "Boo Boo — there's still
an important job to do. Will you please bring our guest
into the Park?"

Boo Boo opened his mouth, and then the Ranger said, "No questions, Boo Boo — just escort our guest into the Park." Boo Boo closed his mouth and trotted off.

All the animals started buzzing at once. Who could it be? A movie star? A football player? The Governor? An astronaut?

And then, in a few minutes, Boo Boo came back, holding the hand of a very pretty little girl!

"My friends," cried the Superintendent, "let me introduce Miss Maryalice Jones. Miss Jones is a very important person here today. Can you guess why?"

"No!" bellowed all the animals.

"Then, I'll tell you! Today, Miss Maryalice Jones became the ONE MILLIONTH PERSON TO VISIT JELLYSTONE PARK!"

A Christmas Visit

One day Yogi Bear received a letter all the way from Alaska. He opened it and read:

Dear Nephew Yogi,

We would all like to meet the only member of the family who is a television star. Please come to visit us for Christmas. And bring your friend, Boo Boo, with you.

I remain, your Uncle,
Northman Kodiak

P.S.   Aunt Kate and our children Yukon and Klondike say "hello."

"Kodiak," said Boo Boo. "I've never heard that name before. Who are the Kodiaks?"

"The Kodiaks are a very fine old bear family. They all live on Kodiak Island," said Yogi. He gave his large globe a spin. "See, here it is," said Yogi. He pointed out the island to Boo Boo.

"That looks pretty far north, Yogi," said Boo Boo. "Maybe we ought to take fur coats!"

"Silly!" answered Yogi. "You *have* a fur coat, young fellow — and you wear it every day in the year!"

"Oh," said Boo Boo, "I forgot!"

The next morning Yogi and Boo Boo went to the train at Jellystone Station. "Two tickets to Seattle, Washington," said Yogi to the conductor. "Make them two ways please," added Boo Boo. He wanted to be sure they got back to Jellystone Park, the home they both loved so dearly.

The next morning the train arrived in Seattle. Then Yogi and Boo Boo got on the mail steamer bound for Alaska.

Three days later the boat steamed up to the dock at An-chorage, Alaska. Uncle Northman met Yogi and Boo Boo there and off they flew to Kodiak Island in Uncle Northman's big red seaplane.

"Hey, Yogi!" shouted Boo Boo over the roar of the seaplane's engine. "We're *really* up north! That's SNOW down there!"

"Most of that snow stays on the ground almost all year long!" Uncle Northman yelled back.

When they got to the island, Yogi bought a bouquet for his Aunt Kate.

"Two dozen forget-me-nots please," Yogi said.

That night, Yogi, Boo Boo, Uncle Northman, Aunt Kate and the Kodiak twins, Yukon and Klondike, all had a big dinner together.

"That was a delicious meal, Aunt Kate!" said Yogi afterwards. "Now come in by the fire, Yukon and Klondike. I'll tell you some stories about famous Jellystone Park."

The next morning Uncle Northman woke Yogi up.

"What's up, Uncle Northman?" said Yogi, sleepily.

"Tonight is Christmas Eve," replied Uncle Northman. "You, Boo Boo, and I must take the sleigh and get a Christmas tree for the twins."

"My goodness!" said Yogi. "I may be in a little trouble!"

"What's wrong?" asked Uncle Northman.

"All that snow I saw yesterday made me sleepy!" answered Yogi. "Me and Boo Boo always sleep all winter long! Look at young Boo Boo here — he can hardly get his eyes open!"

"I can fix that very quickly," laughed Yogi's uncle. "Just splash some nice Alaskan cold water on your face!"

Yogi and Boo Boo finally got up and had breakfast.

"Better eat a good, big, hearty breakfast!" said Aunt Kate, as she kept bringing food to the table. "It's going to be cold in the woods. This is Alaska, you know!"

"How about the twins, Aunt Kate?" asked Yogi. "Don't they eat breakfast?"

"My stars!" exclaimed Aunt Kate. "They eat enough for an army! But we've all been up for hours. Uncle Northman decided to let you and Boo Boo sleep late because he thought you might be kind of tired from your long trip!"

"Golly, Aunt Kate," said Yogi, "if Uncle Northman hadn't awakened us, I think we'd have just kept right on sleeping till April. We were all set and ready for our regular winter sleep!"

"Well, you're certainly wide awake enough now," said Aunt Kate. "Goodness me — you're pretty good eaters yourselves, you know!"

Uncle Northman, Yogi and Boo Boo went deep into the forest and picked out a fine green spruce tree. They tied the tree onto the sleigh.

Then it began to snow.

"It's really snowing," said Uncle Northman.

"Wonderful!" replied Yogi. "I've been dreaming of a white Christmas."

"Let it snow, let it snow, let it snow," sang Boo Boo.

The snow began to come down faster and faster and thicker and thicker. Pretty soon, Uncle Northman got down from the sleigh, went to the horse's head, grasped the bridle and began to lead the horse through the snow.

"You know," said Yogi, "this is mighty strange country. Yesterday we bought fresh flowers — and today — just look at that snow, would you!"

"Happens all the time around here," cried Uncle Northman. "The weather can change mighty fast here in the north country!"

"I sure wish it would change back again!" said Boo Boo, who was getting cold.

"This looks like a blizzard!" said Yogi.

"It *is* a blizzard," called Uncle Northman.

"Yogi, there's something strange going on," said Boo Boo, "I'm having trouble seeing!"

"I'm having it, too," answered Yogi. "What is it, Uncle?"

"Snow blindness!" said the Alaskan bear. "All this white snow. We're going to have to get under cover and wait out the storm!"

"I saw a cave over there!" cried Yogi. "Let's head for it! When the storm lets up, we can head on back home!"

As soon as they got to the shelter of the cave, everyone stamped their cold feet and brushed the snow off of their thick fur.

"I sure hope this blizzard lets up pretty soon," said Uncle Northman. "We have to get that tree back home or Klondike and Yukon will be awfully disappointed!"

"But we can't find our way back if we all get snowblind!" cried Boo Boo.

"I can take care of that," said Yogi. "I brought sunglasses! I can lead the horse, and you two can ride the sleigh with your eyes shut!"

And that's how they managed to get back to Uncle Northman's house. They would have gotten lost though, except for something Uncle Northman figured out. Because when Yogi started to lead the way, he suddenly realized he didn't *know* the way! He could see all right, but he wasn't sure where the house was! Then Uncle Northman said, "Yogi! You keep leading — and every little while I'll take a quick peek to make sure you're headed right! Let's go!"

They finally arrived home just in time for dinner. Uncle Northman, Boo Boo and Yogi were extra hungry, because they had all missed lunch while they were trying to battle their way back home through the big blizzard that nearly trapped them.

After dinner, the twins went to bed early. Next morning, there was the big tree, all trimmed with glittering balls. Klondike and Yukon opened their presents, and everyone was settling down to enjoy the big day.

And then Boo Boo asked a question which had been on his mind since they were in the cave the day before.

"Yogi," he said, "it's lucky you had those sunglasses along! We might have been stuck in that cave for a week! But, you know, I've never seen you wear sunglasses before — how'd you happen to bring 'em?"

Yogi chuckled. "You can blame it on Uncle Northman," he said.

"Me? What did *I* do?" asked his uncle.

"You said something about me being a television star — and celebrities always seem to wear sunglasses. I brought a pair with me — and then forgot to wear 'em! And you know what — nobody even asked me for an autograph!"

Everyone laughed, and then Yogi said, "Come on, Boo Boo, we have to pack and go home!"

"So soon?" said Aunt Kate. "You just got here!"

"Gotta go home and go to bed," smiled Yogi. "We've missed almost a whole month's sleep already!"

Cindy Bear's Hero

"There!" said Cindy Bear as she put the finishing touch to her honey cake. Cindy was sure that her cake would win first prize in the Jellystone cake-baking contest.

And she sang a little song as she took out her prettiest bonnet.

Soon Cindy was all dressed and ready to meet Yogi.

Proudly carrying her cake, Cindy set off.

"I'll be waiting at the dock," Yogi had promised, "to row you across the Jellystone River."

But when Cindy got there, Yogi was nowhere to be seen. Just then, along came Boo Boo.

"Where is that Yogi?" Cindy asked.

"If I know Yogi, he's taking a nap," replied Boo Boo.

"Well, I'm not going to wait for him," snapped Cindy. Boo Boo cried, "You mustn't go out there by yourself. There's going to be a storm."

"Pooh," said Cindy. "On a day like this? Impossible."

"Please, Cindy, don't go without Yogi," begged Boo Boo.

But Cindy wouldn't listen. She went, leaving Boo Boo saying, "But . . . but . . . but . . ." to nobody at all.

Then off he ran, lickety split!

At the dock, Cindy saw rows and rows of boats.

"I'll take that one," Cindy told the man.

"Don't go out on the river alone, Miss Cindy," warned the boatman. "There's going to be a storm for sure."

"Pooh," said Cindy again. She stepped into the boat, placed her cake carefully on the seat, and rowed away.

Cindy didn't notice the small gray cloud off in the distance.

Boo Boo found Yogi asleep in his cave, and shook him awake.

"Huh?" asked Yogi.

"You didn't meet Cindy as you promised. Now she's out on the river alone!"

"Oh, I forgot!" cried Yogi. He headed for the door in a flash. "Let's dash!"

"Hurry, Yogi, hurry!" pleaded Boo Boo!

Yogi hurried . . . right down to the river's edge.

Not a minute too soon! The little gray cloud had grown big enough to cover the whole sky. The river was all choppy. Far in the distance, Cindy's little boat was rolling this way and that.

"There she is!" cried Boo Boo, pointing ahead.

Quick as a flash, Yogi jumped into a boat! "Yogi Bear to the rescue!" he called as he rowed away.

"Hey, Yogi!" shouted Boo Boo as Yogi's rowboat sped away into the teeth of the storm, "Come back! Come back!"

"Can't stop!" yelled Yogi. "What's the matter?"

"You forgot your rubbers!" shouted Boo Boo. "It's going to be very wet out there! You know what happens every time you get your feet wet!"

"No time to worry about wet feet!" yelled Yogi. "Can you see Cindy's boat?" But Boo Boo didn't answer, because by that time Yogi was pretty far out, and Boo Boo didn't hear him.

"I guess I'll just have to keep rowing, and hope I can find her somehow," thought Yogi to himself.

In the meantime, poor Cindy was having a perfectly terrible time all alone in her rowboat in the storm. The wind was howling, making big, wild waves, and the harder Cindy tried to row, the worse everything got!

Back on shore, Boo Boo dashed to the boatman and shrieked, "Call the Marines! Call the Navy! Call the Coast Guard! *DO* something!"

In *his* rowboat, Yogi was rowing as hard *as he* could, and looking for Cindy at the same time. But the sky was so dark, and the river was so full of waves, no matter how hard he looked he couldn't see Cindy!

The sky was almost as black as night. But when a flash of lightning went C-R-A-C-K and made it almost as bright as day, Cindy saw Yogi.

And at almost exactly the same time, Yogi saw Cindy's boat, bobbing in the distance. Then Yogi really began to row in earnest. He pulled on the oars so hard he almost pulled himself right out of the boat! And gradually, he managed to close the distance between his boat and Cindy's until he was coming very near. And then Cindy made a big mistake!

"Save me, Yogi," Cindy shrieked. And she jumped up and waved her arms.

Poor, foolish Cindy! That was the worst thing she could have done. Her rocking, rolling little boat turned right upside down! With a S-P-L-A-S-H, Cindy and her beautiful cake disappeared under the choppy waves!

"Help!" was the last thing Yogi heard from Cindy, as she vanished.

"Yipe!" said Yogi to himself. "I guess we'll just have to forget the cake — but I gotta save Cindy!"

And then, a little distance away, Cindy's hat bobbed to the surface, and Cindy was under it!

"Oh, my!" thought Yogi. "Here's where I get my feet wet." Then aloud, he cried, "Be brave, I'll save you!"

It wasn't for nothing that Yogi had won first prize for life-saving in his school days.

Cindy's beautiful cake was never seen again. But Yogi's strong arms and sure stroke saved Cindy.

Don't get the idea that it was an easy rescue. Cindy was almost as big as Yogi, and she was frightened, and struggled in the water, and fought Yogi when he tried to take her in a rescue grip. Before he could even *begin* to bring her ashore, he had to calm her down—because a frightened person in the water can drown both himself and the person trying to rescue him!

So Yogi talked to Cindy, and got her quieted down and began the long pull to shore, where his little friend, Boo Boo, was waiting.

Before long, Boo Boo was helping the soaking wet Yogi and Cindy onto dry land.

After they got their breath back, and coughed up a lot of water, and shook themselves sort of dry, Yogi suddenly realized what had caused all of the trouble. He saw Cindy standing there, and moaned, "Golly — it's all my fault! You've ruined your hat, and your dress, and your cake is gone forever, and you almost drowned, and the whole *thing* is my fault! If I hadn't been so doggone lazy and gone to sleep, I would have been on time to meet you, and none of this would have happened!"

"Nonsense!" said Cindy. "Maybe you've forgotten it — but I haven't! Yogi Bear, you saved me from drowning!"

"Golly!" said Boo Boo, "that's right! Yogi, you're a hero!"

"Well, shucks," answered Yogi, "I couldn't let Cindy drown, could I?" And he sneezed three times in a row.

"Bless you!" said Boo Boo and Cindy together.

"Thank you," said Yogi politely. "I think I'd better be getting back home. C'mon, Boo Boo. You guessed it just right — I'm getting a cold from getting my feet wet!"

"OK, Yogi," said Boo Boo. "Let's get going and see if we can do anything about that cold!"

"Nonsense!" said Cindy. "You're both coming straight home with me — I'll take care of you!"

By the time they got back to Cindy's, Yogi was full of shivers and shakes. In no time, Cindy had him wrapped in blankets, with his feet in a tub of hot water, and a hot-water bottle on his head.

Yogi couldn't seem to stop sneezing. Achoo, Achoo, ACHOOOO! And then he'd sigh and say, "Oh dear, oh dear — and the whole thing is my fault!"

From the kitchen, where she was doing something mysterious (but which smelled wonderful), Cindy called, "Yogi, you stop blaming yourself. Just remember you're my special double-extra hero!"

"Some hero," groaned Yogi. "You almost got drowned, I almost got drowned, we lost two rowboats, you ruined your dress and your hat, and your cake is gone forever! And I've got the world's champion head cold!"

"Yes, but if you *hadn't* been a hero," piped up Boo Boo, "you and Cindy wouldn't be here at all!"

"And as far as my lost cake is concerned," went on Cindy, "That's no problem. As a matter of fact, I'm doing something about it right now!"

"Is that what smells so good?" asked Boo Boo.

"A special honey cake for a special hero!" said Cindy.

"Wait — don't bring it in yet!" cried Boo Boo — and dashed from the cave.

"Now where is that little bear going?" wondered Yogi. Boo Boo heard him just before he left the cave and called, "Don't go away! I'll be right back!"

"He sure gets going in a hurry when he wants to!" said Yogi. "Cindy, can you come out of the kitchen for a few minutes? I want to talk to you."

"Yes, Yogi — what is it?" asked Cindy. "Don't make it for long — my cake's almost done!"

"Only take a minute," said Yogi. "I just want you to promise me that you won't take out a boat with a storm coming up any more. It was my fault — but you did something dangerous!"

"You're right, Yogi. I was just very angry and disappointed — and didn't really think about what I was doing. You can be sure I won't ever do it again!"

"Good!" said Yogi. "Glad to hear it. Achoo!"

Just then, Boo Boo came racing into Cindy's cave, out of breath and holding something behind his back.

"All set!" he cried. "How about the cake, Cindy? Is it ready yet?"

"The cake will be ready to come out just as soon as I go to the kitchen and take it out," replied Cindy. "What is all this, anyhow?"

"Bring it in and you'll see," said Boo Boo.

Cindy brought the cake, and Boo Boo said, "Since we have a hero, I have made a medal shaped like a star — for a star hero!"

"And here is a hero's cake," said Cindy.

Yogi tried to say 'thank you' — but all that came out was ACHOO!

The Jellystone Olympics

"Boo Boo, my boy," said Yogi Bear one day to his little chum. "Did I ever tell you how I was nursery school champion?"

"Lots of times, Yogi," said Boo Boo patiently.

"I did? At Miss Minnie's Nursery School?" asked Yogi.

"Lots of times, Yogi," repeated Boo Boo.

"You *sure* I told you? About winning the rock-tossing and boulder-lifting championship?" Yogi went on.

"You told me about NINE MILLION TIMES!" yelled Boo Boo, losing his patience a little.

"Oh," said Yogi. "Well, I just thought I'd tell you, because I'm entered in the Jellystone Olympics! C'mon — I want to go and meet our coach and tell him not to worry about those two events!"

The two bears hurried over to Jellystone Stadium, where a lot of the athletes were practicing.

"Morning, Coach Pheebly," said Yogi. "I've come to tell you that you can stop worrying about rock-tossing and boulder-lifting — I'm a sure winner!"

"Oh, yeah?" said Coach Pheebly. "Well, Mr. Yogi Bear, I don't care how many events you won in nursery school — this is the Olympics! You're in the *big time* now! And let me tell you something else, Mr. Star — you're out of condition! Now, you get going, start practicing, and get back in shape!"

"Yessir," said Yogi. "Right away!"

"And one more thing!" yelled the coach as Yogi and Boo Boo started to leave. "Stay away from honey! You're too fat!"

"Wow, Yogi!" said Boo Boo, as they made their way back home to begin working out, "I guess *he* told *you*!"

"Ahhhh," growled Yogi, "coaches are all alike! They were always after me in college, too! Run some more! Lift some more! Throw some more! They *never* let you rest!"

"Well, you *are* a little bit too fat, I guess," said Boo Boo. "That's probably why he told you no honey!"

"That's another thing!" said Yogi. "What does he know about honey? Honey is *good* for bears! It makes us *strong*!" And just then he saw a very good-looking beehive — one with lots of honey in it. "Watch this! I'll show you!"

"Oh, no you don't!" said Boo Boo. "You heard what the coach said! NO HONEY FOR YOU, YOGI!"

"Oh, grindstones and whiffletrees!" snorted Yogi. "Let's go home and start work! But I'm telling you something right here and now, Boo Boo! There's going to be big trouble if I can't have any honey!"

The two bears went back to their cave home, and a little later in the day, Yogi began to practice for the rock-tossing and boulder-lifting championship events.

He began by tossing very small rocks — not much bigger than pebbles, really. Then he tossed larger ones, until he worked up to where he was tossing pretty big ones — just about the same size as the ones which would be used in the competition. Then he switched to boulders. He lifted and lifted — but when he got to the really big ones — they wouldn't come up!

"Don't worry, Yogi," said Boo. "Keep trying!"

"I *am* trying!" said Yogi. "I just don't seem to have enough strength!"

Every day, on their way to Yogi's practice spot, they passed that same beehive — and it was LOADED with honey! Every day, Yogi's eyes would light up when he saw it. But every day, Boo Boo would say the same thing:

"Remember what Coach Pheebly said, Yogi! NO HONEY — you're still too fat!"

"I'm *not* too fat!" snapped Yogi. "I'm too doggone weak! I need some of that honey to make me strong!"

"No way," Boo Boo would answer. "Train harder!"

So Yogi would toss, and toss, and toss some more — but the rocks weren't flying as far as they should. Then he'd lift, and lift — but the really *big* boulders just wouldn't come up. And the date for the Jellystone Olympics came closer and closer.

Then, one morning — it was THE DAY! It seemed as if everyone in Jellystone was there! Bands paraded, cheerleaders urged the crowd to cheer louder, lots of athletes were prancing up and down the field getting ready to perform in whatever events they were entered. Finally, it was time to begin. The bugler in the band blew a tremendous blast, and the master of ceremonies announced the first event on the long program.

Boo Boo was standing with Coach Pheebly, while the first few contests were run. The coach turned to Boo Boo and said, "How about Yogi, Boo Boo? Has he been training hard?"

"Oh, yes, coach!" answered Boo Boo. "He's been going at it hot and heavy every day. He hasn't missed once!"

"How's he doing?" asked the coach.

"Well," said Boo, "I don't think he's happy about it. He keeps saying he hasn't got all his strength."

"Nonsense!" said Coach Pheebly. "If he's really been training, he'll have all the strength he needs!"

"I dunno," said Boo Boo. "He wants that honey pretty badly! Says that's why he's weak!"

"Gosh!" said the coach. "It's nearly time for his events. Go and get him and bring him here — fast!"

"Ulp!" gasped Boo Boo, who then jumped four feet in the air and came down running!

"Hokey smokey!" he thought to himself. "Where *is* that crazy Yogi? If he's done all this training, and worked so hard — and then forgot to even show up — I just don't know what he'll do!" Then he began to think about where Yogi could be. There were a lot of possibilities, but Boo Boo figured that Yogi had just overslept, so he headed for the cave where he and Yogi lived.

He threw open the door of the cave, yelling "Yogi! Yogi Bear! Get up! It's time for your events!" But Yogi wasn't in the cave, awake *or* asleep!

"Oh, pig's feet and rosebuds!" cried Boo Boo. "Now, I'm gonna have to chase all over Jellystone to find that big sleepyhead. Where? Where? Where can he be sleeping?"

He thought for a bit, then snapped his fingers. "The huckleberry patch!" But when he got to the huckleberry patch — no Yogi. Then he thought some more, and ate a couple of handfuls of huckleberries while he was thinking.

"Maybe — just maybe," he thought, "Yogi decided to go swimming! It doesn't make much sense to get all tired out swimming when you have to toss rocks and lift boulders, but I'd better look!"

So he raced to the swimming hole — but again, no Yogi. And then Boo Boo remembered something. The beehive! The one that was loaded with honey! "Ho, ho!" cried Boo

Boo. He liked the way that sounded so much, he tried it again. "Ho, ho! The beehive!" And he fairly *tore* through the woods, and there was the great rock-tosser and boulder-lifter himself — sound asleep under the tree with the hive on it. Only the hive was no longer on the tree — it was lying on the ground — empty!

"Yogi! Yogi! Wake up!" shrieked Boo Boo.

"Wasssamatter — is it April already?" mumbled Yogi. "Gosh — I just got to sleep!"

"Coach Pheebly will put you to sleep *forever* if you don't get going," yelled Boo Boo. "Your events are coming up — and you've eaten a whole hive full of honey!"

"Don't worry about it," said Yogi. "It just makes me strong!"

"Come ON!" cried Boo Boo.
The two bears hurried over to the big meadow where the Jellystone Olympics were being held. They arrived just as Yogi's first event was being announced.

"Two entries for the boulder-lifting!" announced the master of ceremonies. "Roger Biceps — of the Jellystone Rangers — and Yogi Bear! Mr. Biceps will lift the first boulder!"

"I know this fellow," said Yogi to the coach. "I beat him in nursery school!"

Roger Biceps lifted the first boulder easily. Then Yogi walked up and lifted the same boulder just as easily.

Both contestants lifted the second boulder — but on the next one — Roger Biceps strained and tugged — but he couldn't get it even one inch off the ground. And then, it was Yogi's turn to try to lift it!

"Psst! Coach!" whispered Boo Boo. "I'm scared — Yogi just ate a whole beehive full of honey!"

"Omigosh!" exclaimed the coach. "He's ruined! He'll *never* get that boulder up in the air with all that honey in him!"

Of course, what the coach didn't know was that there *had* to be extra strength for Yogi in all that honey. After all, several hundred hard-working bees had spent two whole months putting all *their* strength into making it!

So Yogi smiled at Coach Pheebly and Boo Boo, and shook his hands over his head at the crowd, and said, "Sorry to do this to you again, Roger." Then he walked over to the big boulder that Roger Biceps couldn't even budge, and lifted it all the way up over his head!

"How about *that,* coach!" cried Yogi, as the crowd cheered wildly. "That's what honey can do for a bear! Before I ate that hive full of honey, I couldn't even have *budged* that boulder!"

"I guess maybe you've got something there," admitted Coach Pheebly. "I don't know how it works — but it sure seemed to do *something*!"

"Maybe," said Boo Boo, "bears are different from people. I mean, I *know* they're different, but I mean about eating — and what kinds of things make them strong!"

"I just hope you haven't used up *all* your strength," said the coach. "You still have the rock-tossing contest — and that Roger Biceps looks like a pretty good tosser to me!"

"Beat him *any* day," said Yogi. "I might even beat him *without* any honey!"

Roger Biceps got ready to toss the first rock.

It was a pretty good, long toss, too. Then he tossed his second, third, fourth and fifth. The crowd gave him a big round of applause.

Now, it was Yogi's turn. The first two tosses were way short.

"Just what I was afraid of," said the coach. "He's used up all his strength!"

Yogi's next two tosses were worse than the first two!

And then Boo Boo saved the day! "Yogi," he called, "come here!" Yogi came over and Boo Boo said, "Just happened to bring along a pot full of honey! Here! Go to it!"

Yogi gobbled up the honey, picked up the last rock and tossed it all the way out of the meadow, over a stream, down a hill and into the Jellystone River!

And that's how Yogi won first prize in the Jellystone Olympics!

Show and Tell in Jellystone Park

One day, Ranger Smith, who was in charge of Jellystone Park, called Yogi into his office and said, "Yogi, I've just received orders from Park Commissioner Phudd. Tomorrow, all the animals are going to have to go to school, and I will be your teacher!"

Yogi didn't like the idea very much, but he asked, "When does school start?"

"Tomorrow," answered the Ranger, "and I'm putting you in charge of telling everyone to be in the classroom at 9 o'clock tomorrow morning!"

Yogi *still* didn't like the idea, but he went out and told everyone, and next morning, the animals assembled in the classroom. The only ones missing were a family of owls who slept all day, two beavers who had bad head colds, and one old, snappy turtle who refused to come out of his shell.

The Ranger started things off by calling the roll. This got very confusing, because all the animals didn't really know their names, and many of them had never even *heard* of school, and didn't know what they were supposed to do there.

Finally the Ranger got everything worked out, and gave out pencils and paper and erasers, and assigned someone to clean the blackboard. Then he said, "That's all for today. Tomorrow, everyone will bring in something for show and tell. Class dismissed!"

As the sun was going down, the Ranger looked out of his window and saw Yogi busily scurrying around.

"My goodness," said the Ranger to himself — "I wonder what Yogi can possibly be doing with all those bottles and boxes? And why is he carrying a lantern? My word! If he's getting together something for show and tell, he's waited a long time! It'll be dark in a little while, and he's just starting out?"

But what Yogi had on his mind was this: he decided that since he was the biggest and probably the smartest in the whole class, he was going to check up on all the rest — and whatever each one did, he would do it better!

In the morning, he was ready!

"Good morning, class," said the Ranger, next morning.

"Good morning, Ranger Smith," replied the class.

"How did you make out with your things for show and tell? Everybody ready?" the Ranger asked.

"Sure! We're ready! You bet! Let's get going!" yelled the class.

"How about you, Yogi?" asked the Ranger. "You seemed very busy yesterday. Did you find something interesting to show the class?"

"Ranger Smith," replied Yogi, "just get this thing started. I promise you I'm going to show you some things you never saw before!"

"Things like what, Yogi?" asked the Ranger, who was really very curious about Yogi's mysterious racing around the day before.

"Oh, no," answered Yogi. "I don't want to go first. Just let anyone you want go first, and then I'll take a turn. Then someone else, and I'll take another turn. OK?"

"Just as I figured," thought the Ranger. "He wants to do it all!" Aloud, he said, "It seems a little strange, but if it's all right with the class, it's all right with me!"

And so, the class voted on it, and decided to go along with Yogi.

"Very well," said the Ranger. "Who's first?" A very small young mouse got to his feet and said "Ahem!" two or three times. He held out a rather large leaf — with a ladybug sitting on it. "I captured this bug," said the mouse, "while she was out walking with another bug, who escaped."

"Oh, no he didn't!" yelled Yogi, popping up. "I have him right here in this bottle. Notice his high silk hat, his umbrella, and his red vest! Now, little old mousie, here, brought in a plain, everyday ladybug. But I have in this bottle the only real, live GENTLEMAN bug ever seen in Jellystone Park — or any other park, for that matter!"

The poor mouse didn't know *what* to say, so he sat down.

But one of his brothers jumped up and shouted, "My turn! My turn!"

"Go ahead," said the Ranger. The mouse walked to the front of the class, staggering under a huge mushroom. "This mushroom," he began, "is the biggest one in the whole park. I discovered it growing all by itself in a cave. It took me almost all night to get it here, it's so big and heavy!"

The Ranger asked, "Are you sure it's a mushroom? It's not one of those poison toadstool things, is it?"

"I don't think so," said the mouse. "As a matter of fact, I nibbled on it two or three times — and as you can see, I'm not sick or anything!"

"Good!" said the Ranger. "We'll award you a nice prize for showing the biggest mushroom!"

"Now, just one ding dang minute!" cried Yogi, leaping to his feet. "I've got something here that makes that mushroom look positively puny!" And he reached under his seat and brought up a big jar.

Everyone crowded around to see what was in the jar. "Stand back, everyone!" ordered Yogi. "Give him air! As you can see, in the jar is a chair, with a real, live frog sitting in it!"

"Very interesting," said the Ranger. "But what's that got to do with mushrooms?"

"Aha!" cried Yogi. "The chair which the frog so kindly consented to sit on is what's left of a mushroom that was twice as big as the other one! I CARVED that chair from the giant mushroom! Can you imagine how big it was before I started carving?"

The Ranger wasn't really sure what to say. Some of the mice were looking angry, and muttering things like 'Foul!' and 'No fair!' Finally the Ranger said, "All right! Cool down! We'll decide about the mushrooms some other time! Who wants to go next?"

"Me!" called Boo Boo. "Have a look!" And he marched to the head of the class and held up something which dripped golden drops.

"It's a honeycomb," said Boo Boo. "Some bees loaned it to me for today! A real honeycomb with real honey!"

"Gosh!" cried the Ranger. "That's a REAL find! I don't think I've ever seen one that size before! Do you get to keep it, Boo Boo?"

"Golly, no!" answered Boo Boo. "I promised the bees I'd bring it back right after school. It's the best honeycomb in the park!"

"That's a great show and tell idea," said the Ranger. "A REAL honeycomb!"

"Well, now," said Yogi, "I have to agree with you. But I just happen to have here something even greater!" And he opened a box he was holding.

"Well, for Pete's sake, Yogi," said Boo Boo and the Ranger together, "What IS that crazy-looking thing?"

"Fellow classmates," began Yogi, "you've just seen Boo Boo's honeycomb. But what I have here is the only honeyBRUSH in the world!"

"Goodness, goshness, Miss Agnes!" cried Boo Boo. "A honey*BRUSH*? Where'd you find it, Yog? I bet not even my bee friends ever saw one of those!"

"I have a bee friend, too," said Yogi. "The QUEEN bee herself! She sat up all night making it out of some honey that was giving her indigestion! So I not only have a honeybrush, but I can keep it — the Queen was glad to get rid of it!"

By this time, everyone in the class was getting a little bit discouraged. The gentleman bug, the giant mushroom chair, and now — a honeybrush. Actually, no one wanted to show and tell ANYthing — because they just knew Yogi would come up with something bigger, or better!

But finally one of the foxes came forward with a beautiful butterfly in two shades of orange, plus some black stripes and white dots. The butterfly was in a net — and the fox said he was going to let the butterfly go as soon as everybody saw it.

"Good idea!" said Yogi. "Let it go!" They opened a window, and the butterfly flew off. "Watch this," said Yogi. He opened a big, big box, and out flew hundreds of butterflies!

The butterflies circled and wheeled, and then suddenly — "You've seen a fox holding a butterfly in a net. Now here is a net made of butterflies, holding a fox!" cried Yogi.

And as the butterflies flew around, they arranged themselves so they made a kind of net around the fox! Then they all flew out the open window!

When the applause died down, (because what Yogi had done was a truly remarkable job of organizing butterflies) the Ranger got to his feet. "Anyone else?" he asked. Since no one wanted to show anything and then have Yogi make them look bad by producing something better, not a soul spoke up.

"Very well," said Ranger Smith. "I don't know whether it's really proper for the teacher to take part in show and tell. But I've brought in this beautiful flower for you all to see. Notice how large the flower is? It's called a sunflower, because it loves the sun."

Yogi popped up again and began opening boxes.

"I have here," he began, "an even *bigger* sunflower!" "Not only that," he continued, "but I also have a moonflower, which loves the moon, and a star apple. That sort of takes care of things in the sky. Here is an earthworm, a Venus flytrap, which loves flies, and finally a bottle of Pluto Water, which *nobody* loves!"

The class just sat there with their mouths open. And then the Ranger spoke up.

"Yogi," he said slowly, "I have to admit it. You have put together a remarkable collection of things for show and tell. I don't agree with the way you did it — because I'm sure some of the animals feel upset because you made them look bad. Don't you agree?"

"I guess so," said Yogi. "I'm sorry if I hurt anyone's feelings."

"Well, then, that's all right," said the Ranger. "When you've hurt someone, it always helps to say you're sorry. Now that's out of the way, how did you ever manage to get all those things together in such a short time? The last I saw of you, it was almost dark, and you hadn't collected *anything*!"

"I'm a little tired," said Yogi. "Mind if I sit in your chair?"

"Be my guest," said the Ranger.

"Thanks," said Yogi. Then he began to explain: "I was up all night! I never went to bed at all! Most of the stuff was easy. Just went out and picked it up. But I had to hunt up some beavers to carve that mushroom chair with their big teeth, and the frog gave me a real hard time. He didn't want to get shut up in the bottle."

"Why not?" asked Boo Boo.

"He had a bad scare when he was a baby tadpole. Some boys caught eleven of his brothers in a bottle and they had him, too — but he managed to get away. So he doesn't like being in a bottle, but I talked him into it!"

"What about that crazy honeybrush?" asked the Ranger. "How'd you manage that?"

"Well," said Yogi, "it wasn't easy. Queen bees are kind of big and fat and lazy. All they do is hang around the hive all the time, while the other bees stuff food into their mouths. So I went to see her and asked politely, and she turned me down. It took me hours — but I finally figured out how to convince her!"

"How?" asked everyone at once.

"I told her," laughed Yogi, "that I was the big KING bee — and if she didn't cooperate, I was gonna kick her out of the hive and get a new wife!"

And it worked!